The Rumor
And How the Truth Sets You Free

DeShawn Snow

Illustrated by: David A. Perrin III

Carpenter's Son Publishing

The Rumor: And How the Truth Sets You Free

© 2012 by DeShawn Snow

Book One in the Lil Shawnee Series

Published by Carpenter's Son Publishing, Franklin, Tennessee

Published in association with Larry Carpenter of Christian Book Services, LLC
www.christianbookservices.com

Cover Design: Stalling Designs

Cover Art and Interior Illustrations: David A. Perrin III

Interior Layout Design: Suzanne Lawing

Printed in the United States of America

978-0-9839876-8-0

Table of Contents

Table of Contents

1 ★ Pajama Problems

It was just like any other day, I guess. It was raining outside, and my dog, Izzie, was barking. I had eaten breakfast with my mom, dad, and little sister. I was just about to enjoy my favorite TV show when the phone rang.

"Shawnee!" My mom called. "Nia is on the phone for you."

Nia? I thought.

Interested, I got off the couch as little Izzie followed at my heels. I took the phone from my mom. She wiped her hands on her apron and smiled.

"Uh, hello?"

"Shawnee, it's Nia." She was a friend from my school, but I really didn't know her all that well.

"Hi!" I said with excitement.

"Hi. I was just calling to make sure everything's all set for the sleepover at Rayna's tonight."

My heart did flips and landed in my stomach. I suddenly felt like I was on a roller-coaster ride. I was new at school—just starting fifth grade—and desperately wanted to make some friends.

"Oh, yeah. Yeah! What time do I need to be there? And what do I—"

"Six o'clock!" she interrupted.

"OK, and . . . "

I stopped talking because all I heard was silence. Nia had already hung up.

I thought that was weird but decided that maybe there was a problem with Nia's line. All I knew was that I had been invited to a sleepover that night and I couldn't wait!

I darted upstairs as fast as lightning as I sang, "I'm making new friends. I'm making new friends." Izzie followed me. I was even more excited about picking out what pajamas I would wear. As I opened the door to my room, Robin, my 5-year-old sister, was playing with my project markers. The worst part was that she was not using a piece of paper, but my favorite pink pajamas—the same pajamas I was planning to wear to the sleepover!

"Hi, Sissy!" she shouted. "I was coloring a new nightie for you!"

"ROBIN!!" I yelled.

My dog jumped at the sound of my scream and looked up at me. Izzie is a fluffy white dog. The breeder said she's a Teacup Shih Tzu. When my sister mastered potty training, my parents agreed to let her name

the dog. She chose "Izzie."

"What?" Robin cried.

Just then, Dad walked in. He had just come in from mowing the yard and taking a shower. He smelled of pine-fresh aftershave. I loved that smell.

"What's going on in here, girls?" he asked.

"Dad, Robin just colored all over my favorite pajamas! I was going to wear them to the sleepover!"

I marched over to Robin and snatched the ruined pajamas from her hands. Then the tears came. Robin cried—loud and long.

"Whoa now, Shawnee, you need to apologize for yanking that away from your sister," Dad said. "And . . . what sleepover?"

I was mad now.

"What? That's not fair! She ruined them! I had a very important sleepover tonight, and now I don't know what to wear!"

I started crying and Robin started crying even louder. My dad told me he would be right back to talk to me about my behavior. I sat on my bed and flopped onto my back.

I closed my eyes and heard a magical sound like tiny crystals falling to the ground.

Then Nevaeh came.

"Shawneeeee . . . " she said in her singsong voice.

"Oh, Nevaeh. It's you!" I said as I sat up.

She stood at the foot of my bed holding her sparkly wand. Nevaeh was very beautiful and had very big thoughts to share. She always seemed to come to me whenever I had  a need-whether I knew it or not-just like a fairy godmother.

"You look awesome," I told her as I propped myself up by the elbows to get a better look.

"Thanks," she said, smiling. She reminded me of the beautiful angels I'd read about in storybooks.

"So do you!" she said as she flicked her wand and made sparkly dust fall over me.

It sounded like tiny crystals falling to the ground.

She folded her arms.

"Shawnee, you know why I'm here, right?"

"No," I said honestly. I didn't remember calling her.

"A moment ago you said you didn't know what to wear, and I've come to tell you to clothe yourself with kindness." She held up her wand again, and the same sparkly dust fell over me.

"To clothe myself in kindness?" I asked, confused.

"I know your sister colored all over your favorite pair of pajamas, but you have to understand that she's only 5. She loves you and was just trying to show you how much. So, clothe yourself with kindness. Kindness is not rude. As a matter of fact, a kind word spoken is like apples of gold on a beautiful silver plate. It's like a gold earring and a sweet-tasting honeycomb. It's sweet to the soul."

I stood there, amazed at what she had said to me. She was right. I wanted my words to be sweet like that. Nevaeh always spoke the most beautiful words.

"But how do I keep myself from being unkind, like when Robin took my pajamas?"

"You count to five and think of these things: *Apples of gold, settings of silver, and a honeycomb; a kind word is sweetness to the soul.* You say that, and you'll be able to be more kind."

"Wow, I like that!"

I thought I would try it, so I said out loud, *"Apples of gold, settings of silver, and a honeycomb; a kind word is sweetness to the soul."*

"There you go, Shawnee! You got it." We sang those words together again and again as we danced around the room.

Then my dad came in.

He heard me singing, *"Apples of gold, settings of silver, and a honeycomb; a kind word is sweetness to the soul."*

"Shawnee . . . What are you doing?"

He laughed a little under his breath, but he tried to hide it. I looked at where Nevaeh stood, and she smiled at me. She waved her wand and disappeared; she always seemed to do that when someone else entered the picture. I could hear a thousand tiny crystals falling to the floor. I looked at my dad and remembered that he couldn't see her. *Would anyone ever see Nevaeh?* I wondered to myself.

"I like the song you were just singing. It has a lot of truth to it. You know your sister loves you very much . . . "

He stopped what he was saying and asked, "What *were* you just singing?" He crossed his arms. My dad is very strong. Sometimes he lifts me with his big arms and swings me around at the park. That is one of my favorite things. I'm almost too big for that now, though!

I sang the song for him again.

"Apples of gold, settings of silver, and a honeycomb; a kind word is sweetness to the soul."

"Where did you learn that?"

"Ne . . . " I began. But I stopped myself. He wouldn't believe me if I told him. He'd think I just had an imaginary friend.

"Just . . . somewhere."

"Well, good. I like what you're singing. Maybe next time, you can remember that song, huh? How 'bout you go talk to your sister?"

I got off the bed and walked across the hall to my sister's room. She was playing with her dolls.

"Robin," I said, "I'm sorry for what I said to you. Thank you for making my pajamas look so pretty." I held them up. There were purple dots and red stars all over.

"I have a sleepover tonight and I think I'll wear them. What do you think about that?"

"I like it," she said as she rocked her baby doll and kissed her. "Amanda, you're a good girl," she said, walking her baby to her cradle.

I turned around, my slipper sliding on the wood floor, and headed back to my room. Dad stood in the doorway, smiling, and then he gave me a hug.

"Good girl. I'm proud of you," he said.

"Thanks," I said, smiling at him, and then I ran into my room excited about what was in store for that evening.

2 ★ Sleepover Setup

As I ran into my room, I thought about something. When the invitations were handed out at school, I didn't get one. I knew who Rayna was but we weren't friends. How was I even supposed to get to her house?

It was as if the phone could read my mind, because just that moment, it rang. My mom answered after the second ring.

"Shawnee!" I heard my mom call from downstairs. "Phone!"

I ran downstairs.

"Hello?"

"Oh, Shawnee, it's Nia. The address is 504 Banks Street, 70034. You can get the directions online."

"OK, but, um . . . "

There was silence once again. I began to wonder what was going on. I had questions, but I was too excited to be making friends to waste any time worrying! I began to think of who might be there. I knew that Rayna and Nia from my science class would be there. I felt flattered that they wanted to be my friends! I turned around to head back to my room, and my mom stood looking at me very sweetly as she wiped her hands on her apron.

"Honey, who was that? You look very excited. What happened? It sounded like the same girl from earlier."

I let out a giant squeal.

"Yeah!" I hopped up and down. "I'm invited to a sleepover! I'm invited to a sleepover!"

I started skipping around the kitchen. Izzie followed me like it was a game.

"Honey, come sit down," Mom said.

So I sat down on the bar stool next to her.
She took off her apron. She was wearing
denim shorts, a blue T-shirt, and flip-flops. I
thought to myself how beautiful my mom is.

"Shawnee, tell me more about this
sleepover. I don't know this new friend
of yours, so it's important that I meet her

parents. I'm not comfortable with you sleeping over tonight until I know more about this friend of yours and her family."

"But, Mom!" I began, tears welling up in my eyes.

"Shawnee, now calm down a bit. You can still go for a few hours. Do you know this girl at all?"

"She's in my science class."

"Oh, that's nice. Have you ever talked with her at lunch or hung out during recess?"

I looked down at my feet. "No."

"Well, I am very happy that you are making friends. You are such a fun person to be around," she said, patting my leg. "What time are you supposed to be there?"

"Six," I mumbled as I looked down at my feet again. I really wanted to sleep over!

"Well, Dad and I have a sitter tonight for Robin. We're going on a date. We can drop you off at six and pick you up at nine."

I was excited, but I really, really, *really* wanted to stay the night.

"Here's a thought," my mom started. "Why don't you go upstairs and plan out what you're going to wear? You can pack your pajamas and maybe they'll put theirs on early. That way it will feel like a sleepover. If you have a great time, we can have a sleepover here in a few weeks."

I laughed to myself as I remembered what had just happened to my favorite pair of pajamas.

For the rest of the day, we did normal rainy Saturday things: a few chores, a few crafts, lunch, and a snack. Then we printed out directions to Rayna's house. That's when I began to get really excited. I had packed my bag earlier, and it was already waiting by the door. I was wearing jeans, white sneakers, and a purple sweater.

The doorbell rang. It was Annie, the babysitter. She was a nice girl. She had red hair, glasses, and always carried loads of books. Dad said she was in law school and that she had to study a lot.

"I don't want you to go!" screamed Robin, but Mom and Dad kissed her and said good-bye. I waved to Annie and sneaked out through the garage door.

We pulled down our driveway and headed

 out. As Dad drove, I read the directions to him from the backseat. We listened to my favorite CD along the way. Everything seemed perfect. It had even stopped raining.

"Turn left at Hudson. Then turn right on Two Thirty-Six," I announced.

"So, Shawnee . . . " Mom began.

"Right on Banks . . . Five-oh-four," I said as clearly as possible.

Mom went on: "If you need anything, please call us. Here is a cell phone to put in your bag."

I took the cell phone and thanked her, but added, "Mom, everything will be fine. Why would I need to call you and Dad?"

"Oh, I'm just saying. If you need anything," she said, unbuckling her seat belt.

The three of us got out of the car in the driveway of 504 Banks Street. The sun had already begun to set. Two giant trees stood tall in front of the house. We walked up the steps to the porch and passed a porch swing. I rang the doorbell and waited anxiously. A woman came to the door.

"Hello," she said. "I'm Linda, Rayna's mom."

She held out her hand and shook my dad and my mom's hands. My dad stood behind me with his hands on my shoulders.

"This is our daughter, Shawnee."

I smiled my biggest smile at her.

"Well, fun. The girls will have fun, won't they?" But her words sounded a bit plain, and she carried only a fraction of a smile.

Rayna and Nia walked up behind Rayna's mom. They were wearing shorts and T-shirts. They were barefoot and held ice cream cones in their hands.

"Hi," I said. I was feeling a bit shy, but I still gave them a warm smile.

"Hi Shawnee!" both girls said with cheer. They sounded much friendlier than on the earlier phone calls from Nia.

"Shawnee tells us that she knows your daughter from science class," my mom said.

"Oh yeah?" Linda said, now chewing her gum quite hard. She acted like she didn't

know anything about me.

"Yes," my mom answered.

She looked at my father and back at Linda. Something felt very strange at that moment, but I wasn't sure what it was.

I looked up at my parents and smiled.

"Well, sweetie," Dad began. "We'll see you in three hours. Remember, if you need *anything* . . . "

"I know. I know," I whispered.

"Nice to meet you," my parents said as they waved good-bye to Linda.

Linda motioned for me to come in. She shut the door behind me. Rayna and Nia started to lead me down the hallway that divided the area into two rooms on the left and two on the right.

"Well girls, Mother is going to be in the den upstairs with Phil. Try not to make too much noise. You can play in the basement," Rayna's mom said.

And with that, she left.

I wonder who Phil is, I thought. But I decided not to ask, since I had just gotten there.

The ice cream that the girls held looked really good, and I wondered if they were going to offer me some. They didn't.

"Come on, Shawnee," said Rayna, an interesting tone in her voice. "It's this way."

We walked down the steps into the basement.

3 ★ Funny Feeling

In the basement there was carpet, a green couch, a wooden table with a TV on it, and a big yellow dog. My dog was much smaller than this one, and I was a little afraid of this dog. I think they could tell because I stood there awkwardly as they sat on the couch to watch The Disney Channel.

"Oh, don't be afraid of Bella," said Nia. "She's a big baby."

"What kind of dog is she?" I asked.

"You don't know?" Rayna asked, in what I thought was a bit of a rude voice.

"She's a Lab."

"A lab?" I asked.

"Yes, kind of like a lab in science class,"

Rayna said. I was pretty sure Rayna meant that in a mocking way. She looked at Nia as if to tell her not to say anything else.

"Oh," I kind of giggled.

I sat down in a giant, old brown EZ chair and placed my bag next to me on the floor. I wasn't sure what to say next. I felt nervous. *Maybe they'll want to change into their pajamas,* I thought.

They finished their ice cream cones while my stomach growled with hunger. I hadn't eaten much at home because I had been so nervous.

Mindless Behavior was performing on the TV. I said, "I like Mindless Behavior. They're—"

"OK. They're OK," Rayna said, now quite rudely, cutting me off.

I didn't really understand what was going on and why she was talking to me so rudely. Then I remembered what Nevaeh had told me, and I said it silently in my mind: *Apples of gold, settings of silver, and a honeycomb; a kind word is sweetness to the soul.*

That is, I *thought* I had sung it in my mind—but apparently I sang it out loud.

"Oh, what song are you singing?" asked Nia. "That sounds pretty."

I felt my cheeks flush with embarrassment.

"Oh, it's just a song I learned when—"

"I made show choir at school," interrupted Rayna. "In fact, I have a solo. It's quite good," she bragged.

Nia looked down at her folded hands in her lap, then she looked up at me.

"So, it's a song you learned?" Nia continued.

"Yeah . . . uh . . . it's—"

Rayna cut in. "I have to rehearse every day. I also have a vocal coach that I meet with twice a week. In fact, I'm so busy singing, I hardly have time to do things, like clean my room. I don't have chores. Our maid does them."

Really confused, I looked at Rayna. Then I looked to Nia, who looked a little upset.

"Oh?" I said.

"Yes," Rayna said flatly. "Which is why *you're* here."

"Which is why I'm here?" I repeated. "What do you mean?"

4 ★ Homework Headache

Nia immediately stood up.

"Shawnee, what's in your bag there?" she asked as she walked toward me.

"Oh, it's just a bag I packed with my pajamas. I wasn't going to get to sleep over since my mom doesn't know Rayna's parents, so I brought it just in case you two changed into your pajamas early."

Rayna acted liked I hadn't said anything.

"Oh, that's fun. I'll go get mine and change too," Nia said.

"What?!" Rayna hissed.

"What?" Nia replied. "I'm just trying to be nice," she said quietly.

"There's a bathroom right there where

27

you can change," Nia said, pointing. She motioned to the door. "You can change first, and when you're done, I'll change too."

Rayna didn't say anything for the moment; she let this plan proceed. So I walked into the bathroom and shut the door. Something very odd was going on. I had a weird feeling about Rayna; it was like she didn't want me here or something. Nia seemed like she was trying to be nice to me, but Rayna acted like she was her boss.

While I sat on the top of the toilet seat looking through my bag, Nevaeh suddenly appeared, looking as beautiful as always.

"Boy, am I glad to see you!" I whispered. "I don't understand what's going on, but that girl in there is kinda mean!"

"Shawnee, sweet Shawnee," Nevaeh said as she waved her wand.

After a minute, she was speaking again. "You have strength—the strength of a soaring eagle. One that soars above all the chickens, roosters, and crows."

"Huh?" I said, a little confused.

"An eagle is a very strong animal. It flies higher than any other bird does. In fact, some eagles have been spotted flying as high as airplanes, and even higher. Their eyesight is wonderful."

"Shawnee!" Rayna knocked. "Hurry up, will you? I need to use the bathroom."

"OK," I answered.

"Remember, you're an eagle," Nevaeh said. "You're strong, and whatever happens, you can fly above any situation."

I was trying to follow what Nevaeh was saying. She always had a beautiful way of putting things, but I had no idea who the chickens, roosters, and crows were or why she called me an eagle.

Then, without my asking the question, Nevaeh answered.

"*Roosters*," whispered Nevaeh, "wish they could fly, but all they do is squawk. And maybe they can fly a little bit, but they can't soar. They only wish they could! Their job is to wake everyone up with their loud rooster calls. They may seem high and mighty, but they're really not—not compared to an eagle!

"*Crows* are another noisy bird. They can fly a little higher, but they still can't soar.

Remember, eagles soar on heights. Even though you may not hear eagles, they're strong and fast. They're able to do great things. Remember, you can soar above any situation at the snap of your fingers."

"Shawnee! What are you doing in there?" Rayna snapped impatiently. She was LOUD.

"OK, one second please," I answered.

"Rayna," Nevaeh continued, "is a big rooster!"

I laughed out loud.

"What are you laughing at?" Rayna barked from behind the door.

"Nothing!" I said, trying to hide my giggle.

"She's all squawk, but all that talk just keeps her flying low to the ground. No matter what, you are kind, remember? And you are a strong and mighty eagle. Don't forget!"

She smiled as she disappeared, leaving her sparkly dust behind.

I changed into my pajamas and opened the door with a spring in my step.

"What are you so giddy about?" asked Rayna coldly.

I shrugged my shoulders as I walked back to the brown chair.

"Oh, nothing. I'm just a happy person."

"No one is *just* a happy person," she sniffed.

Nia grabbed her bag to change in the bathroom. She looked confused by all of this. *Maybe Nia likes being around happy people,* I thought. *And maybe Rayna just isn't very happy.*

My confidence shone like a bright star in the sky as I eased back into my chair. Rayna studied me. Then she saw the purple stars on my pajamas.

"What are those?" she harassed.

"Oh, my sister designed these."

"She *designed* them?" She was mocking now.

"Yep."

I began to wiggle my toes. *I wonder if they like to paint their toenails*, I thought. *Maybe I should bring up the subject.*

Nia walked out of the bathroom.

"What do you mean? She just colored on them?" Rayna was prying now.

"Aww, that's so cute!" Nia said. "How old

is she?"

"Nia! Gosh, you're always butting into other people's business."

I looked up at Nia, who was pouting like a puppy that had been scolded for chewing on a shoe. Nia had done nothing wrong, and I was beginning to see that Rayna was not a happy person. I wondered why. Maybe Nevaeh could come and talk to her too. That would be a sight!

"Robin is 5 and you should see the rest of her work," I said with as much charm as I could muster. "So, do you girls want to paint your toenails? I brought nail polish."

"I love to paint my toenails!" exclaimed Nia.

"Great, I have lots of colors," I said as I began to unzip my bag.

Rayna had had enough—she was ready to lay it all out.

"Lots of colors, huh?" Rayna began.

"Yes," I said, unaware of what was coming next.

Nia looked at Rayna as if pleading with her not to say what she would say next. But, it came anyway.

"Listen, Shawnee, as I said earlier, I'm a really busy girl. I'm going to be a major singer one day—like Beyoncé—and I'm going to go to the performing arts school. Singing is my life."

She began walking around as she talked.

"That's great," I said with honesty.

"So . . . you know the assignment we were given at school? You know, the one about building a solar system?"

"Yeah . . . "

"Well, I need you to make mine for me, and I need you to make it perfect. I need an A."

I tried to speak, but I couldn't get in a word edgewise.

"I need it in a week."

"What?" I asked in disbelief. "Are you serious?"

I began sliding up to the edge of the chair. Nia began to speak.

"Zip it, Nia." Rayna turned back to me.

"If you don't help me, I'll never speak to you again, and I'll spread awful rumors about you, and you'll never make any friends. Ever. I'm the most popular girl in school. If I say you're a nobody, you're a nobody, and your reputation is ruined."

Something rose up inside of me. I knew I was not a *nobody*. I was *somebody*!

Instead of just keeping it inside, I boldly spoke my mind.

5 ★ Big Bully

"I'm not a *nobody*. I'm a *somebody*!" I said with confidence.

I was surprised at myself. My talk with Nevaeh must have really stuck.

Nia stood by the door, right where she'd been since Rayna told her to "zip it." She seemed afraid to move. It was pretty obvious she had never taken Rayna on like this.

I guessed that there were times she probably wished she had, or could.

Rayna filled the room with laughter as she shook her head.

"Who do you think you are, new girl?"

I wanted to say something mean and ask her who she thought she was, bossing people around. But I remembered the song about kindness I had learned that day and I thought about how to be calm.

"You know, I think I'm just going to go home," I said calmly.

"You big baby!" Rayna teased in a whining voice. "You're going to go home to Mommy and Daddy and *cry*?!?"

I looked for the cell phone in my bag, and I got up to go call my parents.

"I need some privacy, so I'm just going to go back upstairs and call my parents."

"I'm serious Shawnee. You better do my science project, or there will be problems," Rayna said as she followed me to the stairs.

I turned around.

"What even makes you think I'd do a good job? Huh?" I asked, honestly.

"Because if you didn't, your life would be over. I'll tell everyone at school that you're a big baby, and that you have this awful, contagious disease where if someone comes close to you, they can catch it and will never be able to get rid of it for a year. I'll also say that the only reason why you're at this school is because someone in a very high position made a special case for you to be here."

"Are you serious?" I blinked my eyes several times in confusion. "Do you *really* think people will believe that?"

"I am Rayna Sullivan. What I say goes! People listen to me because I *own* fifth grade."

I sighed and put my bag over my shoulder and began to walk up the stairs.

"Bye, Nia," I said. "Thanks for calling me today to invite me."

"She didn't want to," Rayna shot back as she folded her arms. She stared at me with the eyes of a tiger, fierce and fixed on its prey. "I made her. This was all a trick to get you to do my science project. She doesn't even like you!"

"But . . . " Nia began, but didn't finish.

Rayna just glared at me. My heart felt heavy. It sank to my stomach. I could feel tears welling up in my eyes, but I was not

going to let her see me cry, so I continued
walking up the stairs to the big foyer. I
walked over and sat down on the wooden
bench in the hallway. I saw my reflection in
the large mirror across from the bench.

Nevaeh appeared in the mirror.
"Remember, you're an eagle. You can fly
above any situation." She smiled and waved
her wand at me.

I heard footsteps behind me; they were loud and fast.

"What do you think you're doing?" Rayna asked.

"I'm calling my parents," I said.

"You're not allowed in this house anymore, so if you're going to call someone, do it *outside*!" she yelled as she opened the door to the porch.

"But I'm in my pajamas!"

"But I'm in my pajamas!" she mimicked in a singsong voice. "That is what everyone will hear at school. That you're such a baby and you wear baby pajamas with stars colored on them by a 5 year old."

At that moment, I realized that Rayna was the meanest girl I had ever met in my life.

"Fine. I'll go outside," I said, not giving in to her game.

The door slammed. It was 7:30, so it was chilly, and the sun was beginning to go down. I sat on the wooden swing and called my parents. As I opened the cell phone, she opened the door one last time. All I could see was her face.

"You better do it, Shawnee! I know how

to get what I want. I'm warning you."

She slammed the door.

I felt a weird feeling inside. It was fear, anger, and sadness all mixed together. I started to cry. I just wanted to go home, hold my dog, and curl up on the couch. My dad answered the phone.

"Shawnee? Is everything OK? It's just seven-thirty."

I tried to fight back my tears, but I couldn't. "No." I was fighting back sniffles. "Can you come get me? Everything's *not* OK."

"I'm sorry, honey. We'll be right there. We're only about ten minutes away. We just need to pay our dinner bill. Do you want to tell me what happened?"

I didn't feel like talking about it right now.

"No." I wiped my tears with the palms of my hands.

"OK," he said softly. "Well, would you like me to stay on the phone with you until we get there?"

"No, that's OK."

"OK, honey, we're on our way. Love you."

"Love you too," I said as I closed the cell phone.

I leaned back on the wooden porch swing and pushed my feet on the floor to swing. I closed my eyes and leaned back. *All I wanted was real friends. Why was that so hard to find?*

6 ★ Airborne Ailment

Monday morning was just like any other morning. My mom made my favorite breakfast of pancakes and bacon. I even heard my favorite Justin Bieber song on the radio.

But when I noticed someone had opened my locker at school, everything changed.

I'm not sure how someone was able to open it, because there was a lock on it. We all had padlocks on our lockers. And when I looked inside, I noticed a doctor's mask hanging on the hook. *This is weird*, I thought. I took the mask off of the hook and noticed red words written on a note pinned just above the mask:

"Do my science
project or everyone
around school
will be wearing these."

I was shocked and a little confused about what it meant. I did know *who* the mask was from, though - Rayna. I was more concerned with how she had opened my locker than anything else.

It got even worse when I got to science class. I was sitting at my desk minding my own business, and I overheard a conversation at the table behind me with Rayna and a few other students.

"How do you know about this illness?" the quiet girl, who never speaks in our class, asked Rayna.

"I know a lot of inside stuff. You know, from my dad." Everyone around the science table looked at Rayna and listened so intently that you would have thought she was teaching a lab about mixing fun potions.

One boy had his hand on his head, eyes wide open. Nothing ever seemed to amuse this boy, but he seemed really interested in what Rayna had to say today.

"Well, it's called an airborne illness. I'm not sure where this particular person picked up this case . . . "

"Do you know who the person is?" asked one girl.

"Not yet," Rayna answered. "It hasn't been officially released by the government.

Anyway, it's this new, sleepy airborne illness. You get really tired, and then you can't even go to school anymore because you're so tired. Your tonsils swell and you can't eat anything but soup."

"I've had my tonsils removed," said a different girl, "and I like eating ice cream every day."

"It's *not* the same thing," Rayna corrected her. "You can't eat anything cold. It has to be all hot. So ice cream is not allowed."

"This is interesting," another boy said. "And how long does this illness last?"

"A year."

"A year?!?"

"Yes, a year. That's why you don't want to

48

catch it."

"Why haven't I heard of this before?" asked another girl.

"Because you don't know everything going on in the government. A lot of stuff goes on and I know everything because of my dad. All U.S. government officials are briefed on this airborne case."

"Briefed?" asked another kid.

Rayna ignored him.

"I knew one girl who had this illness, and she failed a grade and got so skinny because all she ate was soup. Anyway, I have this mask . . . "

She pulled out of her backpack the very same kind of mask I had found in my locker.

"You wear this because it keeps you from catching the airborne illness."

"What is *airborne*?" asked still another kid.

Rayna rolled her eyes. "It means you can catch it through the air."

"Then why don't you wear it in here?" said one of the boys.

"Because we're not walking and it can't travel as fast when you sit down."

"Oh, I see," said the boy.

Then Ms. Jones, our science teacher, walked in. "Hey, hey, hey! What is going on in here? Why so loud? You all are too hyper for a Monday," she said as she clapped her hands.

I liked Ms. Jones. She was so funny.

Rayna made eye contact with me as she delivered her final words to her audience in a lower voice.

"Any day now, they'll release who is spreading this illness. If I were you, I'd start wearing these masks."

Then Ms. Jones began her lesson. I felt like I had been outside in the hot sun. My face grew incredibly red and I felt like I was sweating. My heart started to race and I felt sick to my stomach. I started to grow nervous. Was it possible for Rayna to convince other people of this fake illness? I guess she could!

My mind started racing. I couldn't let the school go crazy with worry about some disease. I knew one thing for sure: I had to do her project!

"Shawnee? Shawnee?" Ms. Jones said.

I shook my head and remembered where I was. *Oh no*, I thought. *I must have spaced out.*

"I just asked the class a question and you shook your head no."

All eyes were on me and my face grew even hotter! I was so embarrassed. There was no doubt: I'd be doing Rayna's science project.

7 ★ Milky Way Mess

It was almost time for dinner, and I was still in my room gluing Jupiter to a black poster board. Izzie kept trying to sniff the other planets on the board.

"Izzie, no!" I said as I tried to shoo her away. I didn't want the glue to get on her fur. But she didn't listen. The planets seemed to interest her more than my warnings.

I couldn't blame her. If I were a dog, I'm sure I'd want to play with the science board too. It looked good!

Just then, my worst fear came true. Izzie crouched for a moment and then leaped onto the board! She trampled through the glitter *and* the glue. She walked over the Milky

Way and started to bite into Mars, which looked a lot like her favorite ball.

"NO!" I yelled. "MOM!" I shouted toward the kitchen.

I reached down to get Izzie, but her little paws were stuck to the board. OH NO!

I picked her up, and the board came up with her. I guess I had been so wrapped up in thought about school and Rayna that I hadn't realized how long she had been standing on the Milky Way.

And I just kept picturing the whole school wearing those masks.

"MOM!!" I yelled again at the top of my lungs. "Izzie's stuck to my science project!!"

Poor Izzie started barking. She kept trying to free herself, and I could tell this was going to be painful.

Finally, Mom made it to my room. She rushed to Izzie and giggled a little. She picked up our furry friend and kissed her on the head.

"Poor little thing," she said dramatically.

It was pretty funny looking. Mom held Izzie high and examined the giant poster board stuck to her little paws. I hadn't

realized the glue was that strong.

"Honey, run downstairs and have your father call the vet."

I ran downstairs as fast as I could to find Dad. He was outside, pushing Robin on the swing.

"DAD! Come quick!" I yelled across the yard.

"What's wrong, hon?"

I ran over to the privacy fence that separated us from our neighbors. I knew they couldn't see us girls through the fence, but they must have heard us plenty of times. We could get loud playing on the wooden playground set or chasing Izzie.

"Izzie's stuck on my science project, and you have to call the vet now!" I screamed.

By the time Robin and I had run upstairs, Mom had cut the science project board up into tiny pieces. Now Izzie had only small rectangles of paper attached to her paws. They looked a little like dog skis.

When I saw Rayna's project scattered across the wooden floor in my room, I gasped. I must have looked like I had seen a ghost.

"Rayna's science project," I muttered in disbelief.

"What's that, Shawnee?" asked my mom. She cradled Izzie in one of her arms like a baby.

She didn't immediately follow up on her question, but got distracted. "Honey, can you get her some treats from downstairs? The poor little thing is traumatized."

Izzie whimpered and tried to break free from my mom. Robin jumped up and down chanting, "I can do it! I'll go get them!"

She flew out of the room as fast as lightning.

Dad walked quickly into the bedroom, went straight through to the bathroom, and turned the water on in the bathtub.

"The vet's coming over," Dad announced. "He said that, in the meantime, little Izzie here needs to stay in the warm bathtub to try and soften up her paws." He added a bit of soap to the water.

"Mom," my dad called. "Bring in the little princess."

Robin ran up the stairs as fast as she could, all the while yelling, "Izzie, I'm coming! Poor little girl!"

"Poor Izzie!" I chimed in.

Izzie looked pitiful in the warm water. The bubbles started to form and she started to inspect them. Robin fed Izzie her treats and Izzie seemed to cheer up a little. She tried to jump out of the bathtub, but both my mom and dad kept her in. I leaned against the wall, and my sister sat on the cabinet.

"Be careful, Robin," Mom said.

Then, my mom returned to my earlier statement. Moms have a way of doing that.

"Shawnee, I thought you finished your project and turned it in early on Tuesday?"

I gulped—hard. *What should I say?* I asked myself. I had to think fast.

"Yeah," agreed Dad, his arms folded as he looked at me. Mom held on to Izzie.

"Well . . . uh . . . " I stammered. I remembered it had rained really hard on Tuesday and I considered using that as an excuse. But I remembered that Mom had helped me carry the project and we had parked under the special covered entry. She practically carried it into the school. So that wouldn't work.

"I . . ."

I watched the bubbles in the water. And
then . . . I saw Nevaeh's face float up in a
bubble. My eyes must have gotten as big as
saucers.

"Tell the truth. The truth will set you free,
Shawnee!" She smiled and winked.

"What?" I asked, shocked. "How will I be
free? Free from what?"

"What?" Dad and Mom asked at the same
time before looking at each other.

I sat down on the pink fuzzy toilet seat cover.

I decided I had better get this over with. I had better do the right thing.

"I am doing Rayna's project. She made me do it," I said quickly.

"What?" my mom and dad both asked again, and then again looked at each other.

"Yeah . . ." I said as I looked down at my feet.

Mom let go of Izzie and she jumped out of the bathtub. She ran as best as she could, but with her paws stuck, all she did was slide around on the tile. We couldn't help it—we all laughed at her.

"Poor Izzie! We're so sorry!" Mom said.

She picked Izzie up again, and Dad got a towel for her.

"Shawnee, we'll talk about this later tonight after we take care of Izzie, OK?"

Finally, *later* came. The vet had come and gone, and Izzie was back to normal and napping in her dog bed. Robin was already in bed. It was just Mom, Dad, and me at the table. We were all eating cookies and cream-flavored ice cream.

"What a night!" Mom sighed.

I took a bite of the creamy treat.

"Yeah. Poor Izzie just had to step on . . . "

I stopped myself. I was hoping they had forgotten about Rayna's science project.

"Now Shawnee, why on earth would you want to do someone's project for them?" asked my dad.

"Well, I just want friends," I answered honestly. "Plus, she practically made me! She was going to lie to the whole school if I didn't."

My mom put her hand over mine. "Shawnee, you never have to do someone else's homework for them to like you. That's not a true friend. A true friend likes you because of who you are. Not because of what you can do for them."

"Yeah, well, she is going to tell the whole school I have some airborne illness."

My dad laughed. "Airborne, huh?"

"Yeah, it travels in the air. Anyway, she told my whole science class, and she put this doctor's mask in my locker, saying that if I didn't do her project, the whole school would be wearing masks because of me."

My parents both laughed. Then looked at each other. Mom turned back to me. "Shawnee, I'm sorry we're laughing, but she has some nerve and some big imagination there. Perhaps she should use that creativity and do her own project!"

I sank down in my seat. I didn't feel like eating anymore. They saw the look on my face.

"Honey, you just do what is right," Dad added. "The cream always rises to the top. Always keep doing what's right, even when the wrong thing is happening. The truth always comes out."

I went to bed that night thinking of what my Dad had said. The truth always comes out. I guess I'd find out at school just how true that was!

8 ★ Tall Tales

When I got to school the next day, my stomach was full of a hundred butterflies. I tried to stay in the bathroom to avoid Rayna. Just as I adjusted my ponytail in the mirror, Nevaeh appeared.

"Shawnee, don't get nervous, and don't be afraid! You should be brave. You need to be strong! There is no reason to fear. The truth always comes out."

"Have you been talking to my dad?" I asked. That was the same thing he had said!

"No, but it is the truth, and the truth will always set you free."

"Nevaeh, tell me something funny. I need to laugh right now!"

"OK. Well, I'll tell you a funny story about someone who did the wrong thing to get ahead and ended up in a low place!

"There once was a girl named Kelly who went to an all girls private school. At this particular school, a contest took place. There was a ballot box in which all the girls in the school could vote for who they thought was the nicest. The person they voted for would become president of the student council. Now, Kelly really wanted to be the winner of this contest. The winner would receive a lot of fun prizes and the power to make decisions for her grade.

"Everyone was allowed one vote. But while no one was looking, Kelly sneaked her name into the ballot box more than fifty times.

"This didn't go unseen. There was a hidden camera near the ballot box."

I laughed. Nevaeh's story was getting good! It reminded me of Rayna.

A girl walked in the bathroom and went into a stall. I waited for her to leave before I asked to hear the rest of the story. Finally, the girl washed her hands and left.

Nevaeh appeared in the mirror again.

"OK, keep going! What happened?" I asked.

"The next day, the principal of the school found out what was going on and called Kelly into her office. She asked her, 'What prizes do you think the girl who gets the most votes should receive?'

"Kelly thought to herself and grew very excited because she was just sure the principal was talking about her!

"So she said, 'First, order the winner and her friends some pizza for lunch at school. Then bring ice cream sundaes for dessert. Next, have a limousine pick the girls up and take them ice skating!'

"Then Kelly got even more creative, thinking of all the things she'd like.

"'Finally, give the winner a shopping spree at her favorite store.'"

"The principal smiled warmly. 'Anything else?'

"'Yes!'" Kelly added. 'Announce the winner, the person who is elected president of the student council, in the local newspaper and on the school speaker.'

"The principal nodded her head.

"The next day at school, the principal called Kelly into her office, which smelled like pizza.

"Kelly's eyes grew really big. *This is it! The moment I've been waiting for!* she thought to herself.

"'Kelly, I'd like you to take this pizza,

please . . .'

"Kelly started jumping up and down with excitement.

"' . . . and drop it off at Amanda Jones's table. She's the winner of the student's choice award.'

"'But, I . . .'

"'You will then serve the girls ice cream. Afterward, please come back to my office and make a very special announcement on the school speaker that Amanda is the winner, and list the page that she will be featured on in the local newspaper. Also, let everyone know that as a grand prize, Amanda will receive a gift card to her favorite store as well as a limo ride with some friends to the ice-skating rink.'

"Kelly was upset, but she did as she was told. After all, these things were all her ideas and she thought they would happen to her!

"So, be confident Shawnee," Nevaeh reminded me. "Do what's right. The truth always comes out!" She winked at me and waved her wand. And then, with her sparkly dust, she was gone.

What a story! I was more determined than

ever to do what's right. The truth always comes out! I walked out of the school bathroom with confidence.

Rayna was waiting for me at my locker. There was nothing else for me to do but walk to my locker. I couldn't turn and walk away.

"Where's my science project?" she demanded.

"It . . . " I began.

She folded her arms and glared at me.

"It got . . . " My heart was beating fast. I reminded myself that the truth always comes out. That calmed my nerves.

"I don't have to do it," I said boldly.

"What?" she asked, tilting her head to the side. She looked shocked. You could tell she wasn't used to being told no—by anyone.

"I don't have to do it."

"You'll be sorry, Shawnee."

Then, at the top of her lungs, Rayna yelled, "Shawnee is the one! She's the one with the disease! Don't go near her!" She was pointing at me with crazy eyes, and then she grabbed her mask and put it on. I froze in my tracks. I quickly looked at the other students, who stopped in their tracks too.

"I . . . "

Rayna yelled, "Run, everyone!" She ran as quickly as she could away from me.

I was left standing there. There was nothing I could do but walk away.

The whispers started. I honestly didn't care because, at the least, my science project was done, and it was done early! Besides, the truth would come out!

By lunch, the entire school seemed to be wearing masks, pointing, whispering, and looking at me. I was sitting by myself, eating my chips, when Nia came and sat across from me.

"Rayna doesn't have you wearing a mask?" I asked.

"No," she said with a smile.

"You're not afraid you're going to catch the disease?" I tried not to laugh. Nia beat me to it. We both laughed. It seemed the whole school was watching us.

"Shawnee, I wanted to tell you that I'm sorry for the way Rayna treated you last week at her house. I . . . "

"You don't have to say anything else, Nia.

I like you. The truth always comes out," I said, smiling.

At two o'clock, we had a school assembly, and our principal spoke.

"Boys and girls, I have called a school assembly because fifteen of your fellow classmates left school early today because of some make-believe illness."

Everyone looked at each other.

"Shawnee Graves, please come forward, dear."

I froze! Oh. My. Goodness.

"It's OK, sweetie. Come up here, please."

I walked up the steps and onto the stage. The principal patted my shoulder and covered the microphone.

"You're OK, dear. I'm terribly sorry."

I saw what seemed like hundreds of faces looking at me.

"Will Rayna Sullivan please come up here, as well?" Principal Michaels emphasized the *as well* part.

Rayna hesitated, then tried to hide her face as she slumped down in her chair.

"Rayna, I see you from up here. You have no choice. Either come up here or face suspension."

Rayna walked slowly up the stairs.

"I think you owe someone an apology and the school an explanation of your story."

Rayna sighed heavily into the microphone. It screeched and caused the entire gymnasium to cringe. The students covered their ears.

"I'm sorry, Shawnee." She was the worst actress ever. Everyone knew she didn't mean what she had just said. That apology was lame!

Behind the microphone, Principal Michaels asked, "And what are you sorry for?"

"I made up a lie about Shawnee. There is no disease. It's all made up."

Everyone in our school started chattering loudly. What a buzz! Everyone was asking questions like, "Can you believe it?" and "Why?"

"That's right," Principal Michaels said. "This is all a made-up story. Fifteen of your fellow classmates left school early because of this lie. Rayna will have to stay and face detention for two weeks straight."

"But I have voice lessons and show choir! The talent show is coming!" Rayna answered, shock on her face.

Principal Michaels finished his sentence. "She will go to detention every day after school for two weeks, as will anyone else who pulls a stunt like this."

He continued. "In the future, I hope all of you will not believe everything you hear and will make our new students feel welcomed. Teachers, please lead your classes back to your rooms."

Everyone left the gymnasium, still talking about the news.

"Shawnee, I am very sorry about what was said," Principal Michaels said, turning back toward me. "The counselor will call your parents, and we'll all have a nice meeting tomorrow and discuss your big surprise." He had a warm smile on his face.

I thanked him and headed out of the gym.

9 ★ Shawnee's Sleepover

"I heard that Rayna told Shawnee to do her science project," one kid said.

"I heard it was her math homework," said another.

"That new girl Shawnee must be so smart," said another girl.

As I walked to my science class, Nia called after me. "Shawnee! Wait up!"

I turned around. As I waited for Nia and another girl I had never seen before, everyone in the hallway was looking at me—but this time, their looks seemed different. Warm, accepting.

"I'm sorry, Shawnee!" one student said.

"I like your sweater," said another.

"You're really smart!" said another.

It was then that I realized the whole school knew who I was. I was no longer known as the new girl! *Maybe this has all turned out to be a good thing*, I said to myself.

"Shawnee, this is Rebecca," Nia said as she introduced a new friend to me.

"Hi," I said. "Nice to meet you."

Nia laughed. "Guess what, Shawnee."

"What?"

"Do you know the one thing we all have in common?"

"What's that?"

"Rayna asked all of us to do her homework!"

"I'm in Rayna's spelling and reading class," Rebecca giggled, her blue eyes sparkling.

I just smiled and shook my head.

"Hey, we should all eat lunch together tomorrow," I suggested.

Nia and Rebecca smiled and nodded their heads. "Yeah! It would be fun," Nia said. "Let's do it."

Ms. Parks, our history teacher, walked

down the hall. "Come on, boys and girls. Get to your classes."

We waved good-bye and each went to our classes. My next class was science; Rayna wasn't there. I heard other students say that she felt sick and had told the nurse she'd fainted. We all know what really happened. She was embarrassed and found a way to get out of school. Her dad had to pick her up and she was probably at home doing her late science project!

At dinner that night, I asked my mom and dad if I could have a sleepover on Saturday. They agreed and said they'd like to talk to my friends' parents. If they allowed their daughters to come over, they were welcome to, mom and dad said.

"What are you friends' names?" Mom asked.

"Nia and Rebecca," I said as I took a bite of my fettuccini Alfredo.

"And you won't believe what we all have in common!"

"What's that?" Dad asked.

"We were all bullied into doing Rayna's homework!"

My parents both laughed. And then looked at each other. (They seem to do that a lot!)

"Well, there's good news, Shawnee," Mom said. "You finally get to have your own sleepover!"

"Principal Michaels also called," Dad said.

"Oh?"

"We're all going to have a meeting tomorrow morning at eleven with the school counselor to discuss what happened at school today," Mom said. "There might also be a big surprise, I hear."

10 ★ Best Buddies

Eleven o'clock came, and so did the meeting with the counselor. She was a very nice woman with a very nice voice. Principal Michaels was there too. After he apologized to my parents and said how glad he was that we were at the school, he gave me the most unbelievable surprise!

I was allowed to choose two friends to join me in missing the second half of a school day next week to go ice skating with our school counselor! All they would need was signed permission slips from their parents. This was just like the story Nevaeh had told me!

I knew exactly whom I wanted to invite.

Nia and Rebecca, of course! I was so excited to get to lunch. I had double good news.

"Guess what!" I told my new friends as I opened my lunch bag. "My mom said it's OK for the two of you to come over for a sleepover tomorrow night."

Nia and Rebecca's eyes lit up. "How totally cool!" Nia said.

"Yeah!" Rebecca said.

"I just need to give you my number so your parents can call my mom and talk about it."

I gave them my number and told them I'd see them tomorrow night at six. I thought back to Nevaeh's story about Kelly and then said, "And we're going to eat pizza and ice cream! Guess what else?"

"What!?" they asked, the eagerness written all over their faces.

"You two have to go to the counselor's office."

Their faces fell. "Why?"

"To get permission slips to miss the second half of the day next week and go ice skating with the school counselor and me!"

They both looked at me, shocked with excitement.

"Are you serious? I love ice skating!" Nia nearly shouted.

"Me too!" said Rebecca.

"Well, that makes three of us!" I added.

After lunch, we headed to science class. That's when I found out that I had earned an A+ on my project.

Rayna sat at her desk, but she didn't look like the same girl. I felt a little compassion for her. She didn't look at me, and that was OK. I faced forward at my desk and smiled. I couldn't wait until tomorrow.

I didn't have to wait long, but Saturday night still couldn't come fast enough! Both Nia and Rebecca's parents were able to call my mom. Everything worked out for them to sleep over.

I had everything planned out for the evening. First we'd eat pizza. Then we'd paint our toenails. Then we'd change into our pajamas. Then we'd watch a movie and eat ice cream.

Nevaeh was right: the truth always comes out and will always set you free! So free that I get to go ice skating next week with my two new friends!

About the Author

"Together we can create stepping stones that create success and opportunities for every girl."

~ DeShawn Snow

DeShawn Snow has emerged in the entertainment world as a relentless philanthropist, dedicated businesswoman, a television personality, author and busy mother of three boys. Best known for her starring role on the first season of BRAVO's hit television series "The Real Housewives of Atlanta," Snow has continued to build her career after leaving the show.

Snow is the President and CEO of DeShawn Snow Enterprises (DSE) and DeShawn & the Boys Productions (DBP). DSE's offices oversee the entertainment division of Snow's organization, including business development, media management and the creation and distribution of novelty brand merchandising. This division is also the originator of several books currently in production. DBP is a springboard for the media revolution that Snow has established to create quality entertainment with integrity.

Snow currently splits her time between Los Angeles and Atlanta, where she is developing projects and spearheading various charities, including the DeShawn Snow Foundation, which furthers her commitment to women of all ages. In addition to her business ventures, Snow is very active in her faith. As a minister at New Birth Missionary Baptist Church, Snow endeavors to help others find hope in a world of hopelessness while spreading the unconditional love of Jesus.

Visit Lil Shawnee and all of her friends at
www.lilshawnee.com

Keep up with Lil Shawnee and her friends

Keeping Up With the
Joneses: And How
Love Is All You Need

978-0-9839876-5-9

Taking Center Stage:
And How to Really
Shine From Within

978-0-9839876-9-7

Here's a sneak peak at Lil Shawnee's newest adventure in Book Two, *Keeping Up With the Joneses.*

1 ★ Shiny Things

"Wow! Look at that!" I said to Rebecca.

My friends Nia and Rebecca and I were arranging our sleeping areas for our slumber party. Nia brought the softest blanket I had ever touched and unfolded it over my living room couch. It was pink, with fluffy down feathers in it. It felt amazing!

Rebecca shouted, "I want to feel it!" She stood up beside the couch with her arms out wide and fell backward onto the blanket. Her body sank into the softness.

"Wow! This is like . . . clouds!" she said.

I wanted to feel it too, so Rebecca got up and it was my turn to fall back onto the blanket. It felt like I was landing on cotton candy!

"If this were mine, I'd never sleep in my own bed!" I said dreamily.

Nia sat on the edge of the couch and gave us a look. Something about that grin told us that her bed at home was even better.

She explained that her bed was a *Tempur-Pedic*.

"A temper? . . . " I asked.

"Pedic," she finished for me.

"They're like a thousand dollars," she added.

"Whoa!" I said.

Our conversation was interrupted when my mom came into the living room with hot-buttered popcorn.

"Thanks, Mom!"

"Thanks, Mrs. Graves!" chimed my two friends.

"Need anything else, girls?" my mom asked.

"No thanks, Mom," I answered. "I think we're good!"

Nia looked upset, though.

"Nia, are you OK?" I asked.

"Yeah, Shawnee," she said cheerfully,

before quickly putting her smile back on.

Hmmm . . . That's strange. Something's up, I thought to myself.

I got up off the sofa and put in the new Justin Bieber DVD.

"Have you two seen the movie?" I asked with excitement.

They answered at the same time.

"No!" Rebecca said.

"Yes," said Nia.

"Oh, cool! I just love Justin Bieber! He's coming to town tomorrow for a concert," I said.

I lay back down on my red blanket and blue pillow. Rebecca cuddled into her sleeping bag while Nia lounged on her cloud-like bed.

"It would be so awesome to go!" Rebecca said as she grabbed a handful of popcorn and stuffed it into her mouth.

"The most awesome! And I think I would faint if I got his autograph!" I said as I grabbed my own handful to munch on.

Nia sat quietly as she looked at her heavenly blanket—the blanket that felt like clouds.

I sat there imagining that clouds must feel like silk. When I snapped out of my daydream, I noticed that Nia was wearing the same strange expression as before.

This time, though, I wasn't the only one who noticed. Rebecca saw the look too.

"What's wrong, Nia?" Rebecca asked.

"Oh, nothing," Nia muttered.

She looked at the popcorn. She took a handful. She breathed a big sigh. Rebecca and I waited for her to speak. This was taking forever!

Nia started, "It's just that I have tickets to that concert and . . . "

We didn't even give her a chance to finish her sentence before we both jumped up; we must have looked like rockets launching.

"What! Are you serious? Are you for real?" we both asked.

Izzie, my fluffy white dog, bolted her little body into the living room to investigate. The poor little thing was now getting along quite well, considering that last week she had super glue all over her paws!

"That's the coolest thing ever!" I said as I picked up Izzie and swung her around.

"Yeah," Nia said plainly, as if she were bored with the whole subject. It was like someone had asked her if it was raining. She just didn't seem to care.

As if it could get worse, she answered flatly, "Yeah, front row and backstage passes."

You would have thought Rebecca and I had won a million dollars, because we both jumped up and down screaming, "Oh my gosh! Are you serious?"

We were way past excited. Izzie played at my feet and tried to jump to my knees while Rebecca moved her jumping to the couch.

Nia just answered with another flat "Yeah."

"Yeah? Uh . . . yeah? That's all you can say?" I asked.

"Yeah!" added Rebecca.

"It's . . . nothing. It's just, I know it seems really cool and everything, but I'd rather go with, you know, my mom and dad. They never have time to do anything with me, so they send my nanny instead."

Why does that matter? It's Justin Bieber! I'm sure they could come another time!